Tell Me a Real Adoption Story

by Betty Jean Lifton
illustrated by Claire A. Nivola

Alfred A. Knopf　　New York

Day School

THIS IS A BORZOI BOOK
PUBLISHED BY ALFRED A. KNOPF, INC.

Library of Congress Cataloging-in-Publication Data
Lifton, Betty Jean.
Tell me a real adoption story/by Betty Jean Lifton;
illustrated by Claire A. Nivola.
p. cm.
Summary: A parent tells an adopted child about
coming into the family.
ISBN 0-679-80629-6 (trade)   ISBN 0-679-90629-0 (lib. bdg.)
[1. Adoption–Fiction.] I. Nivola, Claire A., ill. II. Title.
PZ7.L6225Te 1993 [E]–dc20 90-26506

Designed by Mina Greenstein
Manufactured in the United States of America
1 3 5 7 9 10 8 6 4 2

For Sam Gross, my young adviser,
who has his own real story,
and for his sister, Annie

Tell me an adoption story.
Again?
Yes, again.
Then will you go to sleep?
Yes, then I'll go to sleep.

All right. How about this—

Once upon a time there was a fisherman and his wife who found a baby near a rock on the riverbank.

No, not that one. I want something I haven't heard before.

Very well, here's a new one.

Once upon a time there was a King and a Queen,
and they lived in a big palace with a dog and a cat.

Like our dog and cat?

Yes, just like them. But the King and Queen were
very sad because they didn't have the one thing they
wanted. You know what that was?

A baby.

That's right. And so they sent their wise men all through the kingdom to ask if anyone knew where they could find a baby.

Did anyone know?
No one knew. The King and
Queen grew sadder and sadder.

And then one day an old fortuneteller appeared at the palace gates and said she had something to tell the King and Queen. The guards were about to turn her away, when the royal couple passed by.

"Let her come in," they told the guard.

Did she come in?

Yes.

What did she tell them?

She said: "If you take your carriage to the orange grove that is just beyond the lake on the edge of your kingdom, you will find what you need to be happy."

And so the King and Queen put the dog and the cat into the carriage. And they rode and rode and rode to the orange grove just beyond the lake at the edge of their kingdom. And do you know what they found?

A baby.

That's right. There, under an orange tree, they found a very tiny baby.

Where did the baby come from?

What do you mean?

How did it get under the tree?

Oh, I don't know. That's not important.

Why not?

Because what's important is that the baby reached out its arms to the King and Queen, and they knew it wanted to belong to them. They picked it up and took it back to the palace with the dog and the cat. And they all lived happily ever after.

Is that all?

Yes, that's all. And now it's time to go to sleep.

But where did the baby come from?

I told you, I don't know.

I think I know.

I don't like that story.

Why not?

It was all make-believe. Tell me a <u>real</u> adoption story.

What's real?

A story about me.

That was about you—in a way.

What are you doing under there?
I'm <u>never</u> coming out.
Never?
Not until you tell me a <u>real</u> story.
Please come out.
<u>*No*</u>*.*
I think I have the story you want.
You promise not to make anything up?
I promise.

Where should I begin?

At the beginning.

Here goes—a *real* story—from the beginning:

Once, not too many years ago, there was a *real* woman and a *real* man.

Like you and Daddy?

Yes, exactly like us. And they had a *real*, cozy house.
Like ours?
Yes, exactly like ours. And they had a *real* dog and a *real* cat.
Like our dog and cat?
Yes, exactly like ours. But they didn't have the one thing they wanted—a *real* child.
A child like me?
Exactly like you.
Go on.

And so they asked everyone they knew where they could find a baby. They asked doctors and they asked lawyers, they asked friends and they asked strangers, and they asked adoption experts if they knew.

Did they ask a fortuneteller?

Well, they found someone who was just like a fortuneteller because she knew a young woman who was about to have a baby.

Was that me?

Yes, that was you.

You mean I wasn't in your tummy, Mommy?

No, I wish you were. But you were in your other mother's tummy. As soon as we heard about you, Daddy and I went to meet her.

You met her!

Yes. We were very lucky. Sometimes mommies and daddies aren't able to meet the mothers of their babies.

What did she look like?

She looked very much like you.

Then what happened?

Then you were born. Daddy and I went to the hospital and your other mommy placed you in our arms.

Was she sad?

She was very sad because she couldn't take care of you.

Did she cry?

Yes, she cried. And Daddy and I cried. We all cried together.

Why did you and Daddy cry?

Because we knew how much we wanted you, but we also knew how much your other mommy would miss you. And then we all hugged and kissed each other. And held each other tight.

Did she say anything?

She said she loved you very much. And would never forget you.

Did I cry?

No, you didn't cry.

What did I do?

You slept, all snuggled up in a warm blanket.

Go on.

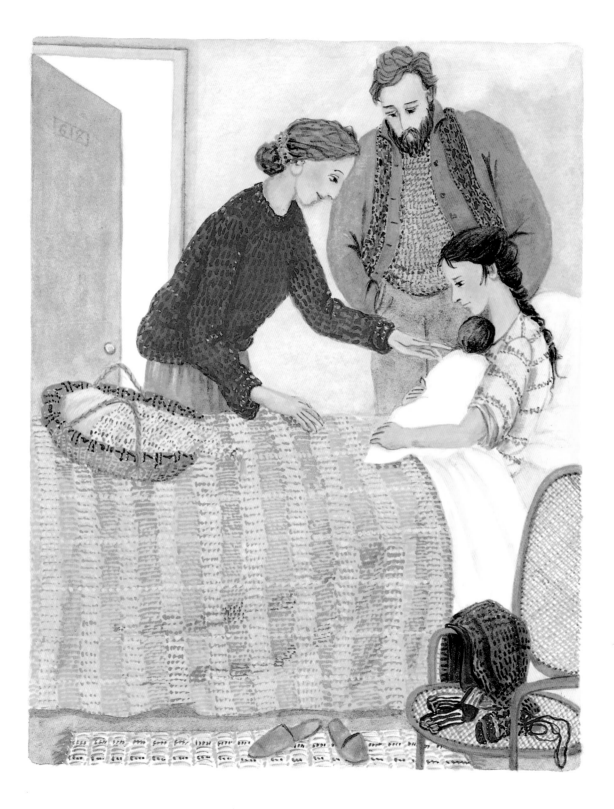

Then Daddy and I brought you home. I still remember the dog and cat were waiting by the door to welcome you. They sniffed you all over — and you seemed to like it. We sent your other mommy some pictures of us all together.

You did?

Yes. And you grew and grew and grew into the very size that you are today.

Where is my other mommy now?

I'm not sure.

I wonder if she ever thinks of me.

I'll bet she does. Do you ever think about her?

Sometimes. Why couldn't she take care of me?

She wanted to. But it wasn't possible for her or your other daddy.

Why not?

Maybe someday you can ask her.

I'd like to see her picture.

Daddy and I can try to arrange that. She'd probably like to see your picture now, too.

I'll make her a drawing of me in my room with my cat and dog.

That's a wonderful idea.

And I'll make one for my other daddy, too.

I'm going to sleep now.
I'll open the window.
Open it wide.

Did you like the story?
Yes!
Why?
Because it's <u>my</u> story. It's really about me.